CW00860129

Kim Temple was born and raised in Hertfordshire and has always loved children's books. She had a book displayed in an Art exhibition when she was just ten years old. Years later after repeatedly being told to put pen to paper due to her wonderfully creative childlike imagination, this book was born. She currently lives with her daughter in Cambridgeshire. She loves writing, singing, making people laugh...oh, and cake. She really loves cake.

# Jake and the Unexpected Smile

Written and Illustrated
by
Kim Temple

AUSTIN MACAULEY PUBLISHERS™
LONDON • CAMBRIDGE • NEW YORK • SHARJAH

A CIP catalogue record for this title is available from the British Library.

ISBN 9781528981279 (Paperback)
ISBN 9781528981286 (Hardback)
ISBN 9781528981293 (ePub e-book)

www.austinmacauley.com

First Published (2020)
Austin Macauley Publishers Ltd
25 Canada Square
Canary Wharf
London
E14 5LQ

To Payge, we're a team...we've got this.

Thank you to my incredible daughter, Payge, for all her love, help, support, encouragement and laughs. Thank you to my beautiful Mum, for telling me to never give up. Thank you to my sister, Rebecca, for her help with proofreading. Thank you to my dear friend Mark, for always believing in me and thank you to all my family and friends, without whom this book may never have been written.

Do you believe in magic? Do you believe in miracles? Do you have an amazing imagination?

There is a place where your imagination and belief can see the impossible.

Jake was bored. His best friend, Oliver, was away and he just couldn't think of anything to do that would stop his boredom.

"What is that face for?" asked his mother. "If you are bored, you can always help me around the house or tidy your room," she said with a smile.

That's the worst thing Jake could think of doing, he sat there thinking how he'd rather watch his grandad shaving his nose hair than do that.

"I'm going out on my bike, I'll be back before dinner," he said as he grabbed his coat and hat and quickly went out the back door.

It was a cold and crisp day but the sun was shining. He decided to ride to the far end of the street which led to a woodland area that was great for climbing trees and building dens. There was also a small river where he and Oliver had stick races and skimmed small stones to see whose would go the furthest. He really missed Oliver; he made him laugh so much, they always had the best time.

Jake sat against an old willow tree feeling sorry for himself, when he noticed a squirrel that seemed to be trying to bury a carrot. What a strange thing thought Jake whilst watching curiously.

“It’s not that strange really,” said a voice from above Jake’s head.

Jake leapt to his feet and looked up into the dangling branches of the willow tree.

“Who’s up there?! Show yourself!” he shouted.

He picked up a large stick from the ground and poked it into the branches.

“What are you trying to do with that?” said the voice. “And you thought Syril was strange!”

The voice let out a loud bellowing laugh and suddenly the branches parted to reveal a face. Jake was so astounded he almost fell over. The face belonged to the tree and it was smiling at him.

Jake closed his eyes, shook his head and looked again. The face was still there! He rubbed his eyes and slapped his face and looked again. Still there!

“Why are you hitting yourself? Are you mad?” said the tree with a concerned but amused look.

“No I’m not mad!” said Jake. “You can’t be real. I must be dreaming!” And he slapped himself again.

“Stop doing that! People will think you’re crazy! You are not dreaming, I’m William...the wise old willow tree. Now calm yourself down before you knock yourself out,” he laughed.

“I think you’re crazy!” laughed the squirrel.

Now Jake even thought he was crazy. A talking tree and a talking squirrel that was burying a carrot!

“This is Syril the squirrel,” said William. “He has a nut allergy so he eats carrots; although, I keep trying to explain to him that carrots grow in the ground, he really is making too much work for himself by digging them up and then burying them again!”

He let out another bellowing laugh.

"That's the strangest thing I've ever heard...a squirrel allergic to nuts!" laughed Jake.

Syril looked up, "Hey, at least I don't slap myself!" he said, pulling a silly face.

They all started laughing and Jake introduced himself. Suddenly an area of the ground started moving and lifting up. Jake watched curiously until the mound stopped at his feet and then all of a sudden a face popped out. It was a mole that seemed very out of breath, who was dusting the mud off himself.

"Hello," said Jake, crouching down to shake its hand.

"This is Mark," said William. "He is a very clever fellow and keeps a lookout for all of us in the woodlands."

"But aren't moles supposed to be almost blind?" asked Jake.

William laughed.

"You're talking to a tree and you've met a squirrel that is allergic to nuts," he said. "So is it that unbelievable to meet a mole with perfect sight?"

Mark, the mole, smiled and shook Jake's hand.

"Really sorry to interrupt but we have trouble coming!" said Mark, looking very worried. "The large rock is grumbling which can only mean one thing!"

"Dartanyan!" said William and Syril as they looked at each other with concerned faces.

Suddenly, animals started to appear from everywhere. From behind trees, bushes and from the river. They were all talking at once and running about all over the place in sheer panic. Jake had never seen such a sight.

“William! What’s happening?” he shouted, so as to be heard in all the commotion.

“Everybody, be quiet!” bellowed William. “All this chaos won’t get us anywhere!”

There was an immediate hush and stillness as all the animals stopped in their tracks.

“It’s Dartanyan awakening,” said Mark. “He wants to destroy William and use this land for himself to build a lair. He is an evil dragon who will do anything to get rid of us all.”

Jake was scared and could feel the hair on the back of his neck stand up. I must be brave, he thought whilst wishing that Oliver was standing next to him as he always knew what to do when things were scary.

Then out of nowhere Jake heard the sound of guitars. He looked over to where the music was coming from and saw a badger playing one guitar and a peacock playing bass. This is getting weirder and weirder, thought Jake.

The badger was called Brian and was an excellent guitarist and the peacock was called Payge and she rocked the bass. Female peacocks are normally very plain in colour but Payge was so colourful and beautiful. Jake now understood that anything was possible here.

“You all need to calm down,” said Brian as he leant his guitar against a tree.

“Yes,” said Payge. “There is only one Dartanyan but there are many of us, if we all stick together I’m sure we can come up with a way to defeat him.”

Jake looked around at all the creatures and noticed that all of them had something unusual and quirky about them.

William: a talking willow tree.

Syril: a squirrel that’s allergic to nuts.

Mark: a mole with great eyesight.

Brian: a badger out during the day, so not nocturnal.

Payge: a female peacock with colourful feathers.

There was also a swan called Sue that had a float under her wing as she couldn't swim, a robin called Russell who didn't like the cold of winter, a skunk called Smelly that actually smelt lovely and many more animals each with their own strange but wonderful traits.

Jake began to wonder what was unusual about Dartanyan.

Suddenly, the ground began to shake and the loudest rumble echoed through the woods. Everybody froze and Jake gasped as the trees began to part. A large creature appeared with terrifying roars. Its body was huge and scaly.

Jake looked up to see its enormous head and angry eyes. It had two horns and very sharp teeth and had clouds of grey smoke bellowing from its nostrils.

The creature stopped in front of William as the other animals ran and hid in bushes and behind trees.

“Well, William, you are still here I see,” it said in a very deep gravelly voice.

“I’m not going anywhere, Dartanyan, I have stood here for hundreds of years, this is my home,” said William. “My roots are deep and you cannot move me.”

“Then I will destroy you!” roared Dartanyan, as he took a deep intake of breath and his eyes glared.

“Stop it! Stop it!” shouted Jake as he ran and stood directly in front of William.

Dartanyan lowered his head and stared directly into Jake’s eyes. Jake could feel his breath on his face, which smelt like disgusting school dinners.

“Well, well, well, what do we have here?” said Dartanyan with a sly smile.

“You really could do with some breath mints,” said Jake as he trembled against William’s trunk.

“Haha! A boy who thinks he is funny!” said Dartanyan sarcastically. “Let’s see how funny you are when I eat you!” he roared.

“Don’t you harm even one hair on that boy’s head!” said William as he lowered his branches around Jake to protect him.

"Attack!" yelled Brian the badger as he ran out brandishing his guitar.

Suddenly, all the animals appeared again. Russell the Robin dropped large twigs on Dartanyan's face; Sue the swan slapped him repeatedly with her float; Payge the peacock displayed her glorious tail in front of Jake to shield him; Syril the squirrel ran up and down Dartanyan's back hitting him with a carrot; Mark the mole threw lumps of mud at him, although he seemed to hate picking the mud up¬; Smelly the skunk sprayed him – which made him smell lovely but stung his skin – and so many other animals were joining in too.

Dartanyan's tail lashed out hitting a tree and leaves were flying everywhere.

"Get off me!" he roared. "You will all pay for this!"

Jake, still leaning against William's trunk, felt his legs shaking.

“Fight!” yelled Syril, using his carrot like a light sabre.

Dartanyan roared again loudly which shook the trees.

“I will be back, William!” he said, “You and your joke of a gang will not stop me from getting what I need!”

“We are not a gang,” said William. “We are friends who stick together and help each other.”

Dartanyan looked at William. Jake noticed a sad look in his eyes. Dartanyan shrugged off the animals, turned and walked away.

“Wow!” said Syril, “That showed him!” and he held his carrot up in the air in triumph.

“Are you okay, Jake?” said William.

FLOAT

Jake was still trembling against William's trunk. He cleared his throat and straightened himself up.

"Yes of course I am," he said, hoping no one could see that he was still a bit shaken.

"It's okay to be scared sometimes," said William, smiling. "It was very brave of you to put yourself between Dartanyan and me. Thank you! Jake."

"Dartanyan is just a big stinky big mouth," giggled Syril the squirrel.

"Why does he want to build his lair here?" asked Jake.

"We don't know; apart from the fact this is a beautiful place that anyone

would love to live in, but for a creature such as Dartanyan, I find it difficult to understand why he would want to," said William.

Jake sat against William's trunk as William and the animals told Jake all about Dartanyan and what had been going on in the woodlands.

"He's gone back to his rock," said Mark the mole, popping out from the ground. "I followed him just to make sure."

All the animals sighed with relief that Dartanyan was gone, for now.

"How about a song?" said Brian the badger, grabbing his guitar.

He and Payge played their guitars, while the animals danced and laughed and even made Jake dance too, which he was a bit embarrassed about at first but was soon laughing as well. After all the dancing and laughing, they all sat down whilst William told wise wonderful stories of magic and wonder, which fascinated Jake.

"It's been a very strange but wonderful afternoon," smiled Jake. "But I should be going home now. Will you all still be here tomorrow?" he asked.

"Yes," said William, "come back tomorrow and we will all be pleased to see you."

"It's lovely that we've made a new friend," said Payge the peacock, displaying her beautiful tail.

Jake smiled and was already really excited to return the next day.

"It's a shame you aren't smaller," said Mark the mole. "I love running and I think you'd love running through underground tunnels with me."

He looked up at William, smiling.

"I think we can sort something out," laughed William.

Jake wasn't sure what he meant by that but he waved goodbye, climbed on his bike and set off home.

The next morning, Jake awoke early wondering if yesterday had been a dream. He leapt out of bed, washed and dressed and rushed downstairs.

"You're up early!" said Jake's mum, surprised she didn't have to go in his room and take his duvet away, which was her normal trick to get him up in the mornings.

"I have to be somewhere," said Jake.

“Not without eating your breakfast first,” said his mum.

Jake sighed and sat down. He ate his breakfast at such a speed, he was lucky that he didn’t get a bellyache.

Finally, Jake was on his way cycling so fast that he arrived at the woodland area in no time at all.

“Hello William! Hello everyone!” he shouted excitedly.

There was no reply. Jake looked around and couldn’t see anyone. He sighed thinking it must all have been a dream after all.

Suddenly, there was a loud, “Charge!” and all the animals rushed out from behind the trees and bushes and ran straight for Jake, almost knocking him over. Jake laughed as Syril the squirrel ran up his body and perched on his head.

“Got you!” laughed Syril.

"Hello Jake," laughed William, parting his branches so Jake could see his smiling face. "Good to see you again," he said.

"Hello William, you all made me jump!" said Jake getting his breath back.

Jake couldn't stop smiling, he'd made great friends and he couldn't wait for his best friend Oliver to come back so he could tell him all about them; although he knew he wouldn't believe him at first.

Mark, the mole, tapped Jake's foot to get his attention.

"So how would you like to come running with me through the underground tunnels today?" he asked.

"But I'm too big to fit in there!" laughed Jake.

"Jake," said William, smiling down, "do you believe in magic? Do you believe anything is possible?"

“I do now after meeting all of you!” laughed Jake.

“Then stand in front of me, close your eyes and imagine yourself as small. Believe in magic as magic only happens to those who truly believe,” said William.

Jake stood in front of William, he closed his eyes and thought about all the magic he had already seen in the woodlands. He imagined himself as small, he really concentrated and kept thinking, I am small. I am small.

“Open your eyes Jake and don’t be afraid,” said William.

Jake slowly opened his eyes and at first all he could see were sparkles glittering in the sunshine. As they cleared, Jake gasped. He was standing next to Mark the mole and they were the same size!

“Whoa! Look at me!” he said with his eyes and mouth open wide in amazement.

"You'd better close your mouth before you swallow any floating dandelion seeds," said Payge the peacock. "Dandelion seeds are for blowing and making wishes, not for swallowing," she laughed.

Jake closed his mouth and smiled. He turned and looked at Mark the mole.

"It's magic!" said Mark beaming. "Fancy tunnel running now?" he laughed.

Before Jake could answer the ground and the trees started shaking and everyone froze with fear. Yet again a loud roar shook the leaves from the trees... it was Dartanyan!

Jake was so small now that Dartanyan looked as big as a house and a hundred times more scary than before. Clouds of grey smoke bellowing again from his

nostrils, his tail lashing and his red eyes glaring like lava from a volcano. His roar was so loud to Jake's now very small ears.

"Quick, Jake, get inside this hole in the ground and stay safe before Dartanyan sees you!" said Mark hurriedly, pointing to a small opening of one of his tunnels.

Jake climbed into the hole just enough so he could still peep out and see what was going on.

"Today is the day, William!" roared Dartanyan. "Say your goodbyes as tonight I will claim this as my home. I am strong and fierce and your deep roots will be no match for me! I will bring you to the ground and use you as wood for my fire!"

"No!" yelled Syril as he ran up Dartanyan's tail, along his scale covered back and to the top of his head where he leant over and poked him hard in the eye with a carrot.

Dartanyan roared with pain and shook his head wildly which sent Syril flying into the air at great speed.

"I wish I was a flying squirrel!" shouted Syril as he tried to extend his arms and save himself. Jake gasped as he thought Syril would be badly hurt or worse but all of a sudden, Russell the robin swooped high into the sky catching Syril and returning him safely to a branch on a tree.

"Wow Russell, that was one hell of a ride!" said Syril. "You are so strong! Can we do that again?"

The other animals giggled and even Jake smiled at how funny Syril was.

"Enough of this madness!" bellowed Dartanyan. "What have you got to say for yourself, William? You are the wise old willow that will be a weeping willow by sunset!" he roared.

"I keep telling you, Dartanyan, that I am not going anywhere. Try as you might you will not uproot me. You are so full of anger and I feel for you. I cannot imagine what a life of anger is like or why you would choose it," said William calmly.

"Yes, why are you such a moody pants? You need to smile more grumpy guts," said Syril.

The animals giggled again but this only angered Dartanyan more.

"You can all laugh now but let's see how funny you think it is when you are all without each other," he growled.

He turned and with a loud roar he left dragging his tail behind him.

Jake climbed out of the hole and couldn't help feeling there was more to Dartanyan than any of them knew. He looked at Mark the mole.

"Mark, I have an idea. Let's go tunnel running, but can you take me through the tunnel that leads to Dartanyan's rock?"

"But why to there?" asked Mark.

"Yes, what are you thinking Jake?" said William.

The animals gathered around Jake curiously.

"I knew you were mad when I first saw you slapping yourself!" said Syril, looking extremely puzzled.

"I just have a hunch about Dartanyan after a few things he has said and I want to see if I'm right. I am very small now and if Mark leads me there, I know I can get close to him without him spotting me," said Jake.

"You could be putting yourself in serious danger," said William.

"Please let me do this, William; I will be so careful, I promise."

William looked down at Jake with a very concerned look.

"Then we will help too," said William. He nodded at all the animals and they knew what to do.

William placed one of his willow leaves on the ground.

"If you stand on this leaf, you will rise into the air. It's like a magic carpet."

Payge the peacock placed one of her tail feathers in front of Jake.

"This feather will make you invisible if you hold onto it."

Syril came forward and laid his carrot down.

"If you are in a dark place, nibble this and you will instantly see clearly."

Brian the badger placed his guitar pick on the ground.

“Hold this and say ‘play’ and you will hear music that will send Dartanyan to sleep for five minutes.”

“Use these items wisely,” said William. “They can each only be used once.”

“Thank you,” said Jake. “But how are myself and Mark meant to carry these items? The peacock feather is very large to carry with all the other things and we are only small and the tunnels are narrow.”

“No fear, Russell is here! And I am very strong!” said Russell the robin as he wrapped his scarf around the items. “I’m going to carry them for you and fly to Dartanyan’s rock. I will meet you there as I can keep hidden high up in a tree.”

“Well, what are we waiting for then?” said Mark. “Let’s go!”

“Keep safe both of you,” said William.

"We will," said Jake as he and Mark leapt into the opening of the tunnel.

Mark led the way with Jake following close behind. The tunnel was narrow but Jake could stand up and run through it. It had many other tunnels leading off in different directions. There were a few worms and bugs but Jake wasn't bothered by them at all and most of them said a friendly hello as they passed by. The tunnel seemed to go on for miles and miles with many twists and turns. Finally Mark stopped as they had arrived at the exit of the tunnel, very close to Dartanyan's rock.

"Catch your breath as now we need to be extra quiet," said Mark.

Jake nodded, calmed his breathing and followed him out of the tunnel.

Jake was surprised at the sight that greeted him. It was a very dark grey place. The sky was cloudy and even the trees were almost bare of leaves, dark and spooky. There didn't seem to be anything growing and no sounds of birds tweeting or any butterflies fluttering around. It was a place that made Jake feel very sad.

"That is Dartanyan's rock," whispered Mark, pointing to a huge black rock almost as tall as the trees.

Jake took a deep breath.

"You stay here Mark and keep a lookout. I'm going over there to have a look."

"No, I'm coming with you," said Mark. "I cannot let you go in there alone."

"Don't forget these, I'll strap them to your back with my scarf Mark," said Russell as he flew down with the leaf, feather, carrot and guitar pick.

KEEP OUT!

Suddenly, Syril appeared too.

“I came here with Russell and we will keep a lookout for you. You didn’t think I’d let you have all the fun did you?” he said with a comic grin.

Jake smiled and was really happy to have these friends with him.

“Right, you two stay high in a tree,” said Jake. “Myself and Mark will see if we can find anything in Dartanyan’s rock.”

Russell and Syril headed to the tree and Jake and Mark crept slowly towards the rock. Jake’s heart was beating very fast and he felt it could burst out at any minute. He took a deep breath as they approached the entrance. It was like a

huge cave which was dark, damp and cold. They crept silently for what seemed like ages, it was as if there was no end to the rock. As they went further they could hear a strange sound which really puzzled them. The closer they got the louder the sound became. They could see light flickering ahead of them.

"Don't make a sound," whispered Mark.

"I'm trying not to," Jake whispered back, "but I feel like he will hear my heartbeat as it's pounding so much."

The flickering light became brighter and they noticed a large figure sat slumped on the ground: Dartanyan.

Dartanyan was sitting by a small fire, his head hung low and the strange sound was coming from him. Jake and Mark looked at each other as they realised the sound was Dartanyan sighing.

"He's sad," said Jake.

"I wonder why?" said Mark. "I've never seen him like this."

The fire was crackling and causing quite a bit of smoke in the already cold and dirty rock. Jake felt his nose tingling.

"Oh no," he said. "I think I'm going to sneeze!"

Mark's face looked horrified.

"No you have to stop it!" he said as he pinched Jake's nose.

The sneezy feeling got worse. "Ahhh, ahhhh..."

"No don't do it, hold it in Jake!" said Mark, panicking.

"Ahhh choo!"

Too late. The sneeze was very loud and the echo in the cave made it even worse. Dartanyan immediately turned his head with such an angry look that it left Jake and Mark no choice.

"Run!" they both shouted and they sped off as fast as they could.

Dartanyan jumped up and with the loudest angriest roar ever he chased them. As Dartanyan was so large this caused the whole rock to shake which made it difficult for Jake and Mark to stay on their feet.

"We don't stand a chance!" yelled Jake.

"He's right behind us!" shouted Mark, turning quickly to see Dartanyan approaching at great speed, his nostrils flaring with grey smoke.

They ran as fast as they could but they were no match for Dartanyan's large steps.

"Mark, give me the guitar pick quick!" said Jake, stopping suddenly.

Mark stopped in his tracks and Jake took the guitar pick from the scarf around Mark's back. He held it up in his hand just as Dartanyan was almost upon them and shouted, "Play!"

Almost immediately, Dartanyan slumped to the ground fast asleep. The snoring was deafening. Jake and Mark looked at each other with huge relief in their eyes. The fire that had been burning must have started to go out as the light was gradually disappearing.

"We need to get out of here now!" shouted Mark, pulling hard at Jake's t-shirt.

"But I can hardly see in this darkness!" said Jake, still trying to catch his breath.

"The carrot!" said Mark. "Nibble on the carrot and be quick as he will only sleep for five minutes and we've probably already lost one of those and if we don't get out now the snoring will probably deafen us for life!"

Jake nibbled on the carrot and magically he could see his way very clearly.

"Let's go!" he shouted so as to be heard over the snoring.

They ran and ran and with each step they were more aware that Dartanyan would wake up soon. Finally they could see the opening to the rock. They both ran out as if their lives depended on it.

"Arghhhhhhh!" they yelled as they came out.

Syril jumped out of his skin and Russell grabbed him so he didn't fall from the tree to the ground. They then hurriedly made their way down to where Jake

and Mark had collapsed on the ground having felt like they'd just ran a marathon.

"What on earth happened in there?" said Russell whilst making sure they were okay and unhurt.

"Yes, what did I miss?" said Syril. "Do you want me to go in there and punch him?" he said, dancing around as if he was in a boxing ring.

Suddenly, the ground began to shake and a loud angry roar came from the rock.

"No time to run!" shouted Mark. "Quick get under the peacock feather!"

They all quickly got under the feather apart from Syril.

"Let me at him!" he shouted, still doing his boxing moves.

The others grabbed him quickly and pulled him under the feather just in time. Thankfully they were now all invisible. Dartanyan appeared from the rock full of rage. His roar shook the whole area and he lashed his tail angrily hitting the trees as he frantically searched for Jake and Mark. He was so enraged at the thought of them getting away that he roared louder and louder and great plumes of grey smoke from his nostrils filled the air. He hit one tree so hard that it came crashing down close to where Jake, Mark, Russell and Syril

were hiding. They all kept so still, completely silent and were very afraid. The sound of the roars, crashing noises and the angry sound of Dartanyan's long tail lashing about was terrifying.

Suddenly there was silence. An eerie silence that scared them even more as they trembled under the feather. Then they heard the sound of Dartanyan's footsteps getting closer until they came to a halt right next to them.

"Stay silent," whispered Russell. "Don't even breathe."

They noticed Syril actually holding his breath.

"Syril, he didn't mean it he just meant be quiet," whispered Jake.

Thankfully and with a sigh of relief, Syril breathed again but very quietly. Dartanyan had spotted the feather and lowered his head to take a closer look. Now they could feel and smell Dartanyan's breath but they daren't move. They knew they were invisible but only while they were holding the feather. They clung to it and to each other.

"Why is there a peacock feather here?" Dartanyan said, not knowing the others could hear him. "Something so beautiful in an ugly place."

Dartanyan carefully picked up the feather and held it up. Jake, Mark, Russell and Syril clung to it with every bit of strength they had as they were lifted higher and higher.

"Beauty has never been close to me," said Dartanyan with a sigh. "I am only surrounded by ugliness."

He returned the feather to the ground and sat down next to it.

"My life is sad, lonely and ugly," he said as he sighed again.

Jake looked at the others and they all had the same sad face after hearing what Dartanyan had said.

"When I count to three," whispered Jake, "Russell, you grab Syril and fly high up a tree and Mark, you give me your hand and hold on tight and we will fly to the top of a tree on the willow leaf William gave us."

They weren't sure what Jake had planned but thought it was a great idea to get further away from Dartanyan and they nodded to agree with the plan.

"One, two, three!"

Up they all flew but Dartanyan spotted them and stood up with a huge roar and tried to grab them in his sharp teeth. He managed to catch hold of the scarf that Mark had wrapped around him but Jake quickly freed the scarf from Mark and they all reached safety, or so they thought.

"Don't panic!" yelled Syril.

Dartanyan ran at the tree causing it to shake as he used all his might to try and bring the tree down.

"Okay, you can panic now!" shouted Syril.

Dartanyan tried again and Russell grabbed Syril and flew to another tree.

Then they realised that each of the items could only be used once so the willow leaf wouldn't fly and save Jake and Mark again. Russell flew back to the tree to save them but even though he managed to get them to the other tree, Dartanyan turned his attention to that one. Again he rammed into the tree determined to get hold of them. They clung to the branches desperately as they all shook with fear.

"Dartanyan!" Jake shouted as loud as possible "We are not here to cause you any trouble! Why were you so sad in the rock?"

Dartanyan ignored him and braced himself to ram the tree again.

"Why were you sad about the peacock feather?" Jake asked, clinging as tight as he could to a branch.

"He's not listening!" shouted Mark, almost losing his grip.

Dartanyan rammed the tree again and they heard the trunk cracking.

"Dartanyan! Listen to me! Why do you talk of ugly things and being alone?" said Jake, trying to hold on to Mark to stop him falling.

"Right, that's it!" said Syril and all of a sudden with the others looking on in horror, he leapt from the tree straight down onto Dartanyan's head.

"LISTEN!" he shouted very loudly in Dartanyan's ear.

Dartanyan stopped suddenly in his tracks.

"Oh no!" said the others fearing the worst.

"You never listen!" said Syril, shouting in Dartanyan's ear. "You just throw your weight around like you're in charge with no thought for anyone else! You're very selfish and rude, your manners are disgusting and it's no surprise that you don't have any friends! If you weren't so big and scary, I'd send you to your room without any dinner!"

Jake, Mark and Russell held their breath after hearing Syril give Dartanyan a good telling off. They also feared what would happen next.

To their surprise, Dartanyan just sat down. Jake could see that he was sad again.

"Russell take me to the ground please," Jake said.

"And me too please," said Mark.

Once on the ground they stood right in front of Dartanyan and Dartanyan didn't seem to care.

Syril was still sat on his head, looking disgusted at the dirt in his ear.

"You need a good bath my friend," he said.

"Friend?" said Dartanyan with a confused look on his face. "You hate me, you all do."

"No," said Jake stepping forward, "we just don't like the things you do. Why are you always so angry?"

"Don't pretend you care," said Dartanyan with a sigh.

"I do care," said Jake nervously stepping even closer. "From what I've heard, you say you don't like living in this place and you don't like being alone."

"Don't pity me!" roared Dartanyan, causing Syril to slip from his head all the way down his back as if it was a slide.

"Wheeeeeee!" said Syril. "Wow, that was fun!"

Dartanyan shook his head but at the same time he almost smiled, almost.

"I don't pity you," said Jake. "I'm trying to understand you. Do you have any friends here at all or friends that come to see you?"

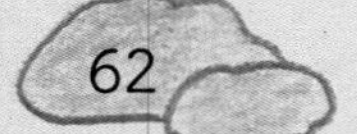

"Who would want to come to this ugly place or be friends with a dragon that can't..." Dartanyan stopped before finishing his sentence.

"Can't what?" said Jake, Mark, Syril and Russell all at the same time.

"It doesn't matter," said Dartanyan, lowering his head.

"It does matter because it's making you sad," said Mark.

"You will all laugh at me," said Dartanyan sadly.

"We won't, I promise," said Jake.

Dartanyan looked at the four of them and although he was afraid they would laugh and it was something he'd never told anyone before, he decided to actually say it.

"I'm a dragon that can't..." he took a deep breath. "I can't...breathe fire," he said, lowering his head in shame.

"Is that it?" said Syril. "That's nothing. I'm a squirrel and I can't eat nuts! Now that's funny, so funny it even makes me laugh! And our friend Sue is a swan who can't swim!"

"I'm a robin so I'm always out in winter and seen on snowy Christmas cards and yet I hate the cold!" said Russell. "How funny is that?!"

"I'm a mole that loves running through underground tunnels but I'll admit I don't like getting muddy and that's ridiculous!" said Mark.

"I never knew that!" said Syril, starting to laugh.

"Me neither!" said Russell.

Mark started to laugh. He had a brilliant laugh which in turn made Jake, Russell and Syril laugh. Then to their surprise Dartanyan started to smile. Such an unexpected handsome smile. Then his smile turned to laughter. His laugh was so loud but so wonderfully charming before long they were all in hysterics.

“Guess what?” said Jake still laughing. “I’m a boy that can’t do fake burps!”

They all stopped still and looked at Jake for a moment. Then they all starting laughing again.

“That’s pure brilliance!” said Mark, holding his belly as it was starting to hurt from all the laughing.

“Too funny!” said Syril now rolling about on the floor in fits of laughter.

“Please stop!” said Dartanyan, who was laughing so much now that the ground was shaking. “I haven’t laughed for years and I’m worried I’ll break wind in a minute!”

“Everyone run away before he farts!” laughed Syril.

Luckily Dartanyan didn’t break wind or fart and the sound of laughter rang through the dark, spooky place that didn’t seem quite so dark and spooky anymore.

"I have an idea," said Jake. "Dartanyan, you must come with us and meet the rest of our friends and make your peace with William."

"I have caused a great deal of trouble there, especially for William," he said. "He would never forgive me for what I've done."

He lowered his head, looking sad again.

"He will forgive you," said Russell. "He has the kindest heart of anyone I know and if he knew how sad you are and how alone you are he would welcome you, I just know it."

"Sometimes," said Jake, "we do things that we are not proud of but to say sorry for those things and showing that you want to change makes all the difference."

"Come on, grumpy," said Syril, nudging him. "You have to let them hear that laugh of yours, but keep your wind in if you can!" he laughed.

Dartanyan looked at the four of them and realised he wasn't looking at four creatures to roar at and scare, he was looking at four friends. He smiled – and wow, he looked so great when he smiled.

The five new friends set off together talking and laughing. Syril, Mark and Jake sat on Dartanyan's back and Russell flew alongside.

When they had almost reached William's woodland, Russell flew on ahead to let William and the others know what had happened and not to be afraid of Dartanyan anymore. Dartanyan was nervous when he arrived and also ashamed of how he had previously behaved. As he walked towards William, the other animals were a little on edge too.

"I do not blame you if you never forgive me, William," he said. "But I am truly sorry that I took my sadness and anger out on you and your friends. I was jealous of you, everyone likes you and you live in a beautiful place. I have behaved terribly and I am very ashamed."

"Wait, sorry to interrupt," said Syril. "Can I use you as a slide again to get down as that was so much fun last time!" he said to Dartanyan.

Dartanyan smiled. "Of course you can," he said.

"Whoohoo!" laughed Syril as he slid down his back, down his tail and flew off the end.

Jake and Mark decided to do the same and they laughed as it really was so much fun. William and the other animals had never seen Dartanyan smile before and it seemed to be catching as they started to smile too.

"Thank you Dartanyan," said William. "Not just for the apology, which was very kind of you, but also for bringing my friends back smiling and laughing. Laughter is one of the best things."

Gradually, if a little nervously, the other animals gathered around Dartanyan and admired how friendly and handsome he looked when he smiled. One by one they all started chatting with Dartanyan.

"William," said Jake, "can you make me normal size again before I go home? I think my mum would pass out from shock seeing me this small, and I won't be able to ride my bike home like this!" He laughed.

William laughed and with a sprinkle of willow leaves Jake was back to normal.

Jake stood there, so happy, that everything had worked out so well and he couldn't wait to bring his best friend, Oliver, to meet all his new and wonderful friends and tell him all about the adventure they'd had.

Dartanyan couldn't stop smiling. He was no longer sad and no longer alone. He didn't need to be angry anymore and that was an amazing feeling for him. He was now making friends to laugh and chat with and he knew this was just the start of many happy memories to be made. The woodland was once again a happy place.

"Hey William, guess what!" said Syril. "Jake can't do fake burps!" And once again he fell on the ground laughing and so did everyone else.

The sound of laughter filled the air and Dartanyan's laugh was the loudest of all.

Jake looked over at William with a smile.

William was right, if you truly believe in magic you will find it, and he had.

## The End